INTEGER

Numbers of the Mind

Edited By Byron Tobolik

First published in Great Britain in 2023 by:

Young Writers
Remus House
Coltsfoot Drive
Peterborough
PE2 9BF
Telephone: 01733 890066
Website: www.youngwriters.co.uk

Printed and bound in the UK by BookPrintingUK
Website: www.bookprintinguk.com
YB0MA0022A

FOREWORD

For our latest competition, Integer, we asked secondary school students to take inspiration from numbers in the world around them and create a story. Whether it's racing against a deadline, cracking a mysterious code, or writing about the significance of a certain date, the authors in this anthology have taken this idea and run with it, writing stories to entertain and inspire. Even the format they were challenged to write within - a mini saga, a story told in just 100 words - shows that numeric influence is all around! With infinite numbers, there are infinite possibilities...

The result is a thrilling and absorbing collection of tales written in a variety of styles, and it's a testament to the creativity of these young authors.

Here at Young Writers it's our aim to inspire the next generation and instill in them a love of creative writing, and what better way than to see their work in print? The imagination and skill within these pages show just a fraction of the writing skill of the next generation, and it's proof that we might just be achieving that aim! Congratulations to each of these fantastic authors, they should be very proud of themselves.

CONTENTS

Hospital & Outreach Education, Northampton

Mahin Miah (16)   38

John Cabot Academy, Kingswood

Ayman Ibrahim (12)   39

Knole Academy, Sevenoaks

Sam Game (11)   40

Loxford School, Ilford

Ibrahim Janjua (13)   41
Roop Singh (11)   42
Haaris Irfan (12)   43

Omagh High School, Omagh

Evan McBrien (13)   44
Jacob Ewing (12)   45

Ormiston Chadwick Academy, Widnes

Harley Parry (11)   46
Rosie May-Bond (12)   47

Ormiston Horizon Academy, Tunstall

Rebecca Roberts (12)   48
Tyler Barnes (12)   49
Sophie Beech (14)   50
Charlotte Plant (13)   51
Daisy Barnett (13)   52
Bethan Jones (13)   53
Keyarna Chinn-Shaw (13)   54
Amylee Colley (12)   55
Sienna-Mae Kinsey (12)   56
Michaela Windsor (13)   57
Lucas Hassall (12)   58

Radnor House Sevenoaks School, Sundridge

Logan Newman (12)   59

Redcar & Cleveland College, Redcar

Cobie Nicholson (15)   60
Leah Ripley (16)   61

Sawtry Village Academy, Huntingdon

Isla Hanlon (13)   62

St Columbanus' College, Bangor

Olivia Smith (14)   63
Ellie Gow (12)   64

St John Henry Newman Catholic School, Carlisle

Evie Bourne (12)   65

St Kevin's College, Lisnaskea

Conor Grew (14)   66

Thamesmead School, Shepperton

Ava Matthews   67

Wigston Academy, Wigston

Naeema Mahmood (13)   68
Esmee Durrant (14)   69
Maia Westgarth Mestre (13)   70
Leah Mistry (13)   71
Allie Wolloff (14)   72
Seth Orton (13)   73
Rhys Moon (13)   74
Riley Liquorish (14)   75
Jayden Williams (13)   76
Arihanna Joseph (13)   77

Logan Lewin (14)	78
Ben Bessant (13)	79
Cadie Munday (13)	80
Olivia Derry (13)	81
Harry Mansfield (11)	82
Jenson Bentley (12)	83
Charlotte Vann (13)	84
Beau Earl (14)	85
Ollie Derbyshire (11)	86
Zaynab Okba (13)	87
Imogen Shipley (11)	88
Isabelle Wall (12)	89
Seth Clamp (11)	90
Matthew Marriott (11)	91
Lily Horton (12)	92

Wilberforce College, Hull

Freya Mower (16)	93
Oliver Rigg (17)	94
Millie Richards (17)	95
Julia Pawlowski (16)	96
Guilherme Barroso (17)	97
Ellis Rennie (17)	98
Luis Witty (16)	99
Cecilia Mukelenge (16)	100
Can Yildiz (17)	101

I WAS PUBLIC
ENEMY
NUMBER 1...

THE
STORIES

Escaped

My great-grandfather was 26 when he was captured in the slave trade. He explained every way of torture and punishment and I'm horrified. On 19th August 1672 he was taken out of the family home. Marched for 2 hours to get to the coast of Africa. Loaded onto the ship with another 200 people took over to the Caribbean. They were force-fed. Diseased or sick slaves were thrown overboard. On arrival they were auctioned off to the highest bidder. My great-grandfather tried to escape, running as fast as he could. Aged 47 he was freed by Scottish abolitionists.

Ciara Harvey (14)
Auchenharvie Academy, Stevenston

Better Luck Next Time

I rolled an 8, the dice glistened in the yellow light. I was doomed. I was going to die because of this stupid dice. The 8-headed serpent slithered towards me, making eye contact as it edged closer and closer, its red eyes glowing in the dark tavern. It hissed in eighths as it coiled around me and started to squeeze me to death. It's 8 months curving into a crooked smile, 8 rows of teeth revealed themselves as the serpent's freaky smile grew as wide as a doorway in a mansion. "Bye-bye," its 8 heads hollered at me.

Jodie Falconer (13)
Auchenharvie Academy, Stevenston

The Vault

They texted me the number of the room, 639. I walked into the room, there was nothing but a note and a vault. The note said: 'Guess the number for the vault'. The vault was big and metal, I couldn't break it. I guessed 639. It was right. It opened, there was a box nearly as big as the vault was. It had a note on it: 'Watch out'. I got a text, 'Open for £630,000'. I opened it, who wouldn't? But then someone jumped out with a knife. I was so surprised, I was set up!

Stella Morrison (13)
Auchenharvie Academy, Stevenston

11pm

It was 11pm and it was very dark. I'd decided to go to a haunted house with my friends. When we got there we had to climb through a smashed window to get in. We were exploring it for ages but nothing had happened yet. That's when we entered the living room. That was a mistake. I pushed the door open and we went in, but we didn't notice what was on the window until we were about to leave and I was the one who saw it. On the window it said *Leave* in bright red blood. We ran.

Gavin Conn (13)

Auchenharvie Academy, Stevenston

My Brother

It was a warm and windy Thursday. I went to the beach. My brother would have loved it.

I found 111 seashells. Maybe it was a sign. I just ignored it for now. On my way home I got a raspberry smoothie, his favourite. His funeral is tomorrow. I really miss him. I asked my mum what time it was, 5:55. She said, "Maybe it's a sign for change."

At his funeral I went up to his casket. The number 999 showed up for a new beginning. He was free from pain and his suffering.

Jane Milne (12)
Auchenharvie Academy, Stevenston

27

It was a cold and rainy night. Me and my best friend decided to take a trip to the Lidl. But then our lives changed forever. We walked in and all we saw was the number 27. An alien came down from the ceiling. It spoke. "My name is 27. Welcome to my home."

Next thing we knew we were in a spacecraft. We said, "Why did you take us?"

But the alien said, "Shut up and sit down. We're in a space race right now."

Then we got home safe and sound.

Alyssa Scrimgeour (13)
Auchenharvie Academy, Stevenston

The Deadly Number 2

There were 2 seconds left till my brother was going to be killed by the police.

2 years later and I now have a husband and 2 kids, but every night something feels off. I hear someone walking around and it's creepy and I feel a presence beside me. But tonight is different. It is 2am. My husband is asleep but a person is speaking to me and I turn the light on and there he is. My brother, alive. He walks over to me and he stabs me. But instead of dying, I scarily wake up.

Mya Davidson (13)

Auchenharvie Academy, Stevenston

I Rolled A 6

It was a Saturday night at exactly 9:08pm. I was with my 2 pals sitting at the living room table. I was currently in jail in Monopoly and I had 1 chance to roll a double or roll a 6. Then it was my turn. I was very nervous. If I didn't roll a double or a 6 I had to pay $50, but I couldn't or I would go bankrupt. I rolled it and it spun across the table. As I checked what I rolled, I cheered as I'd just rolled a 6.

Graeme Baird (13)
Auchenharvie Academy, Stevenston

12 Years Old

I am 12 years old and it's a good age. I liked being 11 but 12 is way better. My name is Millie, my favourite colour is lilac. For my 12th birthday I got £90 and I went to B&M and spent £45. I was down to my last £45. I went to McDonald's and someone stole £5 from my birthday money. They escaped with my money which meant I had only £40 left. I was very upset.

Millie Hall (12)

Auchenharvie Academy, Stevenston

The Last Door

Only 30 seconds left. There were only 4 doors to choose from to meet my perfect utopia or deadly fate. My mind was racing, I couldn't choose. My body was sweating like never before. "20 seconds remaining," echoed through the room. I had to make a decision. I made my choice. Door 3 was the one. I had to go now. I ran towards the door at full speed, my hand latched onto the handle. I swung the door open and the only thing I could see was darkness. My worries swooped in as a gun went off.

Megan Brown (13)
Barnard Castle School, Barnard Castle

Caught

I'm now public enemy number 1. How? The heist was flawless, I have the jewel. I can give it to the people, save them. I make sure to keep moving and stay in the shadows. I didn't set anything off. Wait! Hold on. I think it was that janitor. Did that old crow report me to the government?

Dylan Evans (12)
Blessed Hugh Faringdon Catholic School, Southcote

4 Tulips

I was planting the new tulips I had bought.
"1, 2, 3, 4," I counted.
Later that night, I wondered if I would ever see my sister again - she had been missing for a while now. I thought this as I'd been seeing someone that looked exactly like my sister. Only it couldn't be... She was long gone. I was sure of it. She looked just like her, but the way she was was just so different. So one day I had to check. I dug up the tulips - she was still there. So who was this replica? What did they want?

Koral Owczarenko (12)
Brighouse High School, Brighouse

The Big Heist In NYC

"Only 30 seconds left, we're going to get this safe open, Rio!"
"I know, I can't wait to show NYC not to mess with me and you, Jason!"
"So here's the plan, Rio. We go to the subway and bump it and shoot anyone that gets in our way."
"Yes, sir. Oh, and Jason, if the police come, should we run or shoot?"
"Shoot some and peg it."
"Okay."
"And wherever the train stops get out and get to the garage and show the boss the money and he'll be happy with us. Oh, the safe has stopped ticking. Okay!"

Joel Lam (12)
Copley Academy, Stalybridge

13

I ran through the forest, dodging through the trees surrounding me. It was chasing me. I had no idea what it was. All I remembered was being told, "Be careful, 13." 13... the only name I remembered. It foreshadowed my misfortune. Anything else, name, information, how I got here: gone.

I continued to dash as fast as I could, barely dodging the trees. It was pursuing me and it was getting closer. I was falling, tripping over the cliff in front of me.

Darkness encased me. 13, considered unlucky, the name I'd die with. Or so I thought...

Sage Hickling (13)

Copley Academy, Stalybridge

The Diary Found At The Crime Scene

'9 December 19??' The date is smudged. 'The 9th of the 12th, I've been looking forward to this day for a long time, the anniversary of my experiment. It's going to be joyous. I can't wait! I've been up all night preparing, it's extremely early. I don't think I'm being obsessive as Rogers said - am I? I never had a son so 12 is the next best thing. Honestly, I'm-' The entry ends there. This will be very important. As I look down at the floor to my right I shudder. That poor man... He didn't deserve this.

Tomas Wright (12)

Copley Academy, Stalybridge

There Is Never A Happy Ending

October 13, 1784. It was a dark Friday night at 12 at night and Aria and Emily Blake were playing board games while waiting for their parents to come home. Suddenly there was a knock at the door. Aria answered it.

"Hello, are you Aria Blake?" 2 guys questioned.

"Yes," Aria replied.

The 2 men grabbed Aria and took her to somewhere dark and dreadful. She was locked in a room on her own. She screamed and cried until the asylum master paid her a visit. As he came in with Emily's dead body, Aria fell to the floor distraught.

Chloe Hollingsworth (12)

Copley Academy, Stalybridge

The 13th Mistake

On my way through the dark, blizzardy forest me and my friends ended up stumbling across an abandoned prison called the 13th Mistake. We decided to spend the night as we were lost and had no service. As we entered, a putrid smell clung to our nostrils then we heard a bang and began to explore...

They opened a chamber door when suddenly 3 psychopath cannibals were taking them to a kitchen and chaining them up. Finally, they began scraping layers of skin off us and eating it. The last thing I remember was a pulling then all went dark.

Nikiayia James (12)
Copley Academy, Stalybridge

Apocalypse

I wake up groggily and realise I have to go to school. I try to make myself wake up by telling myself it's my 13th birthday. 20 minutes later I walk downstairs ready for school. "Bye, Mum." She snarls. "Mum?" She turns around, revealing flesh dripping off her face.

I run out the house and see more grotesque humans eating flesh. I assume I am the last man alive in the world. But then I see 13 other people. I race towards them but then a zombie bites.

I wake up groggily and realise I have to go to school.

Archie Taylor (11)
Copley Academy, Stalybridge

House 13

On a dark day, there was a girl walking through the village when she saw a dark house, 13. It looked abandoned but she wasn't sure if it was as it just looked like the curtains were closed. But then she heard a blood-curdling scream... She went closer but the closer she got the more the fog swallowed the house... After some time she finally found it... It was a little vintage house hidden by the trees. She knocked but after no answer, she just walked in. There she saw a tall man in all black...

Jaiden Winterbottom (12)
Copley Academy, Stalybridge

The Girl Who Was Named Eight

In 1894, a girl was born and was named Eight. As she grew up and started school, kids bullied her and made fun of her name.

One day, she felt very upset because she was scared the kids at school would find out the whole family's names. Her mother's name was Twenty and her father was called Thirty. The girl was very confused about why her and her family had such strange names, and she was always wondering why her name couldn't be a regular name. So she began an investigation to find out about her family's strange number names.

Patricia Raluca Varga (12)
Ellesmere Port Catholic High School, Whitby

The Great Fallout

It was the year 2150, 2 years after the AI revolution. Connor was hiding in bunker Charlie, one of the last bunkers in use. The robots, they caused the great fallout.

To him, all was hazy. The only remaining memory was someone being attacked by a robot. The bunker had food that would last for years, but the door was barely holding up. It could fall at any time.

They'd electrocuted everyone on Earth except for him. He was protected. Connor was tasked with finding a way to destroy them, but only if they didn't kill him first.

Luke Cameron (11)
Ellesmere Port Catholic High School, Whitby

The 9 Conflicts That Led To Anarchy

9 is a number that can be good or bad. Bring life or bring death. Make peace or start wars, and bring joy or despair. The date at the time of writing is 2092. A lot has happened in the last half-century. Russia eventually started a nuclear war and, unsurprisingly, lost, which then caused Russia to become a barren wasteland. Kinda like Centurion 3.
The 9th Indo-Chinese war kicked off 2 years ago and India are winning, but only because they have cyber drones. And the 2nd Ameri-Canadian war started in 2049 and is still happening.

Alfie Pattin (14)
Ellesmere Port Catholic High School, Whitby

2:40

2:40, the time that ruined my life! Let me take you back 2 years ago. I was 12. My parents were fast asleep. It was 2:40. The lightning was louder than ever.

I got into bed, snuggling my favourite teddy. Suddenly, a knock from my window. I was curious, but I remembered what my mum said: "Never look out the window at night!" I decided a little peek wouldn't hurt. A shadow stood still. Then I dropped to the ground. I woke up to a bright light leading me to heaven. To this day, I still don't know what happened.

Pixie Owen (11)

Ellesmere Port Catholic High School, Whitby

The Car

As I got into the car, all I heard was, "107." It kept repeating itself. I wondered why it was doing this. I pinched myself to see if it was a dream. It was not.

All of a sudden, the radio said it was not a dream and carried on repeating 107. My mum started going insane. I asked, "Are you okay?"

She looked at me and said, "107."

I tried getting out of the door, it was locked. I started to lose my vision. I was spinning. I repeated the number 107.

Gracie May (11)
Ellesmere Port Catholic High School, Whitby

The Big Birthday Banner

My pigs were 1 on their first birthday and I got all 100 of them a clown and a birthday banner. But Red Fred ate his birthday banner and then he was ill, so I took him to the hospital.

They put him to sleep and cut him open and took the banner out of his belly, then put him back together and woke him up. Then he was crying, so I took him back to the barn.

We had a party and invited all their friends and they opened their presents. I bought him a new birthday banner.

Maddie Maylor Johnston (11)

Ellesmere Port Catholic High School, Whitby

Conquering Death

It is 2099, I am 140 years old. I am conquering death. 2099, a different world. My 140-year-old brain can't scratch the surface of thinking of my past self. 2099 is the year everything changes. Only 2099 humans remain. 2099 is the number of breaths we have. All 2099 people have 2099 breaths. Everyone apart from me. All loved ones perish. Once your identity is found within yourself, the breaths start counting down breath by breath. Then I realise I am 2099!

Freddy Sheedy (12)
Ernest Bevin College, Tooting

The Green Moon Bounty

I was public number 1 victim. I had a bounty on my head for 1 million pounds. My goal was to get past the UK border. When it hit midnight the moon turned green to alert me. I needed a disguise so I bought one for £24. I was 240 miles away. They came after me. When I was 29 miles away they saw me. I ran. Until I was 1 mile away. I used my speed and I made it. I won 1 million pounds. I was amazed.

Tammy Kuges (12)
Ernest Bevin College, Tooting

The Importance Of Number 60

Once, I was 'just' a number. However, this has changed. 60, the ideal number for everyday life, is used for essentials. This includes time. A minute gone to waste is 60 valuable seconds left to rot.

"But why is 60 so important? It's just like other numbers." Well, without 60, you cannot find the equivalent of either a minute or an hour.

Hamza Abdi (13)
Ernest Bevin College, Tooting

The World Cup

I was number 10 for England. It was the World Cup, one more game and the first World Cup final since 1966. I stood as striker, waiting for the whistle. *Breathe in, breathe out...* The whistle went. The clock ticked on 20 minutes, 30 minutes, 40 minutes. Then Brazil was on the attack. 5 seconds left of the first half. I put my head down. *Why this time?* Goal for Brazil. 1-0. Hopes and dreams lost. After half time, 2-0. Come on. The first chance I got a goal. 2-1. Goal. 2-2. One last chance. I struck it. Yes! Goal!

Finley Hastings-Payne (11)
Hobart High School, Loddon

The 5th Of February

"Damn it, Clarence! Can you turn down the noise?! It's bad enough being cooped up in a coffin all day without having to listen to you moan and groan. What's got into you anyway?"

"I'm sorry, Irving. I don't feel so good. My stomach's bothering me."

"You're an idiot. How many times do I have to tell you to choose your victims wisely."

"I'm sorry, Irving. I..."

"Hey! Wait a minute... What's that smell? Clarence, was that you?!"

"I'm sorry, Irving. I..."

And that was the last conversation I had... It was my last memory, the 5th of February.

Ibrahim Ahmed (13)

Holyhead School, Handsworth

Adventure

Just a small trip... Just 5 minutes. I suddenly got knocked out. The blackness covered my vision and I teleported to another life.

It was 22:39. I stared at the location - 29 Pebblestone Road. "So this is it," I mumbled. I stepped on the stairs one by one till I finally got full eye contact with the brown dirty door. I breathed heavily. I couldn't turn back now... Could I? I questioned myself.

I looked left and right. It was buried with broken glass, webs and blood. I shivered as the cold slapped my face... My eyes widened. I was trapped...

Zahra Shah (13)

Holyhead School, Handsworth

Timeline

It was the year 3045. Technology was advanced. These robots knew everything about you. Even if you're unaware of it they can always see you.

I hated this life. I decided to leave the present and time travel into the past. I travelled into the year 1918 thinking how wonderful it could be, but I was wrong. It was a nightmare. Buildings completely destroyed, bullets and bombs raining down. What had I stepped into? I could hear cries and screams but I felt hopeless. Home was a distant memory. Was this God-forsaken place going to be my new normal?

Marija Kolesnikova
Holyhead School, Handsworth

The Unexpected Trap

As our car approached the frightening house I leapt out to walk towards the door. The numbers 787 appeared on the front.

As the door creaked open I could smell rotten flesh on the ground floor. As I walked further I could see something in the distance. I got closer. A huge black figure had appeared out of nowhere.

As fast as a cheetah, I found a door which had the numbers 666. As I walked in I found a little cosy place to hide. But then a loud roar came from behind me.

I ran and made my escape.

Huzaifa Salim (11)

Holyhead School, Handsworth

15

The number 15 stared back at me. My hands trembled and soon became sticky with sweat as the wind blew frantically around me. *Why am I so panicked? It's just a doorknock. Get this nightmare over with*, I told myself.
Anxiously, I lifted my wrist and knocked harshly on the old, rustic door. Silence. Then gunshots. Everything quickly became a blur. Bloodstained windows that had dark, unmoving shadows came quickly into view and all nervousness rushed back at me. I stood frozen, not moving. *Why aren't I moving?* I turned around, but it was too late. Blackness invaded my vision...

Sophie Stewart (13)
Hope Academy, Newton-Le-Willows

13: Bad Luck

The police came rushing into apartment number 13. There had been a murder. Their guns were up, ready to fire. *Bang!* Their quick eyes saw an unexpected, sharp movement. Then suddenly, they saw a little boy outside who they eventually figured out was 13. Then they spotted the boy's mum outside (this was strange as they had not contacted her yet). The final suspect was her boyfriend who was in the wardrobe. They had their 3 suspects. So off they went back to the police station.

On the 13th day of the 13th month, they were shot dead.

Grace Close (11)

Hope Academy, Newton-Le-Willows

Everything Will End Eventually

30 seconds. That was all that was left of my pitiful, misery-inducing life. I took a deep breath, thoughts racing around my mind. I was being hunted and my time was running out. I reached a corner. Dead end. "No, no, no!"

As much as I hated my life, I did value some of it. By some of it, I mean her. Her silky brunette hair and her porcelain skin. Her cute laugh and the way she bit her lip in concentration. As 2 men approached, I knew it was the end. *Bang!*

My final thought was her.

Nevaeh Lewis (12)

Hope Academy, Newton-Le-Willows

6

We gather around the table and roll our dice. 1 of us is not going home tonight. I look at the number sitting before me. 6. I rolled a 6. That 6 will be the reason for my demise. I never should have made that wretched bet. Now, I am doomed. I can't bear to look at that loathsome die, the reason why my life is over. I am going to die. *Bang!* Red. Everything is red. All because of that cursed number 6. Now I'm alone, in solitude, in hell, forever. I'll never forgive and I will never forget.

Elouise Burden (14)

Hope Academy, Newton-Le-Willows

Public Enemy Number 1's Problems

So right there I was caught. I was on the street, public enemy number 1. Arrested for stealing candy from a child, and sentenced to 10 years. In prison, I thought I needed to get myself out. So I used a toothbrush and it eventually worked. I ran but I was caught. I was so close. 20 years in jail this time. I used a piece of broken floor. Once again somehow it worked so I ran again but was caught again. They took pity on me so I jumped with joy. I said, "Thanks!" and made my exit.

Mahin Miah (16)
Hospital & Outreach Education, Northampton

1s And 0s

I was walking to the park until I noticed a cat disappearing into a shed. Investigating the shed, I slipped on a hairball. Flinching about hitting the shed, I fell through the wooden wall. I felt like a ghost. Opening my eyes, I was falling and falling. It felt like I no-clipped out of reality.

I hit the floor, brushing myself off, and I looked up. My pupils widened. All I could see were 1s and 0s. Walking back in shock, I realised that the cat was 1s and 0s too. Then I saw that I was also.

Ayman Ibrahim (12)
John Cabot Academy, Kingswood

The Phonecall

The room was pitch black, the crack in the closet was giving me the only vision but the vision was fearful. A tall man stood at my door. My shaking fingers dialled the people I needed most. 9... 9... 9. His cackled laugh crawled down my spine. The ringing got louder and louder, my heart pounded as he got closer, destroying everything he could. Finally, after what felt like hours, the phone fell quiet.
"999, what's your emergency?" she asked.
"I-" Too afraid to talk. The man got closer, the crack grew bigger and... the call slowly became silent.

Sam Game (11)
Knole Academy, Sevenoaks

1 Minute

We were all covered. All I could think about was reading my duas, reading all of my prayers, and saying sorry to God for all of my sins, but little did I know, it was time to start moving, not talking. The room went dead silent. I heard heavy footsteps. The big, red, petrifying scythe he was carrying was slowly becoming more apparent. A big figure slowly walked intimidatingly towards us. The lights turned on, and we were all laying eyes on a clock... 0:59, 0:58, 0:57... *Bang!* Gunshots were fired from all sides.

Ibrahim Janjua (13)

Loxford School, Ilford

The Beast Inside Me

Today is my 18th birthday and I finally get my element. I am eager but also worried as I may not get royalty lightning. Yesterday I didn't get my power, as I looked up it spelled out c-o-s-m-i-c. I thought it was a myth, this meant I had all elements, I floated as the air around me was a bubble. Fire shot out my mouth and lightning blasted out my mouth. I was the beast.

Roop Singh (11)
Loxford School, Ilford

The End (268)

The aliens had taken over. All the cities, all the roads, all the seas, all the animals, all the continents, all the humans... We had lost all hope, the aliens had 268 million pieces of high-tech bombs planted all around the Earth with each of them counting down... 268, 267, 266...
The aliens had left us to die. 3, 2, 1...

Haaris Irfan (12)
Loxford School, Ilford

The Case Of 2005

It was a dark and stormy night. I had been set my first detective case. Pulling up in my 1999 BMW M5, I stepped out of my car and was hit by a wind so intensely cold it made my skin prickle and my muscles tense. I then proceeded to make my way up the path to what looked like a forgotten, somewhat abandoned mansion.
I crept up the stone steps just to be met with a tall, pale man. He didn't speak. He just seemed to stare. But I had a feeling this was him, the killer of '05.

Evan McBrien (13)
Omagh High School, Omagh

Lost From Reality

The year is 3014. The streets are covered in smog and dull lights from rusty lamps. But we don't see that. We see a fake world, an escape from our world... Almost like we are lost from reality.

It was around 20 years ago and a company known as OKIS had made a new VR headset. It seemed harmless until suddenly in 2096 the servers were hijacked by Xenoz, a terrorist group. And they ruined the lives of millions of innocent people because now you can't take the headset off...

Jacob Ewing (12)
Omagh High School, Omagh

Earth8-99

I am 2. That is us, that is me. We are just numbers. The year? It's 99. I Despise it here, everyone does. We are trapped, alone, kidnapped. Day after day, night after night, more people follow the system. Well, not now. It wasn't until 99 it stopped. He is not like us. He breathes heavily. He is dressed different. He is an odd number.

"Hey, 2! Yes you, come here," he beckons. It is against the rule to listen to another. I slip out, under the cover of darkness. "You know me? Well, I can break the system."

Harley Parry (11)
Ormiston Chadwick Academy, Widnes

The Day Came

One day I woke up in a mysterious lab. It was strange. When I looked won I saw a number on my shirt. It was 2756... When I saw it I thought, *what happened? Why am I here? Who is here?* When I looked up I saw some terrifying people. They looked like monsters. They had horns, tails and wings on them. Suddenly I felt a sharp pain through my whole body, like I was being stabbed. My spine spasmed and wings popped from my back. A figure appeared... "Please help, I don't know what is happening, please help me..."

Rosie May-Bond (12)

Ormiston Chadwick Academy, Widnes

3:33

It crept closer. *Gasp!* Another bad dream. I checked my alarm clock. 3:33.
"I need a drink."
I walked to the kitchen and opened the fridge. *Ring ring.* The phone... What an odd time to call someone. I declined.
"I'm too tired to communicate with anyone."
I picked up a bottle of water. *Ring ring.* I answered, they must've needed to talk to me. An eerie white noise came from the speakers. I hung up and walked to my room. I couldn't sleep... I turned my TV on. *Ring ring.* Again! I answered.
"I'm outside."
Whatever... *Knock, knock.* The door...

Rebecca Roberts (12)
Ormiston Horizon Academy, Tunstall

Mesmerised

Tick, tock, tick, tock. It sat eagerly. "Nearly 12," they squealed, completely mesmerised by the slow ticking of the clock. Its eyes had enormous bags beneath them, deprived of sleep. A wide gaping smile stretched across its face as the seconds ticked down. "Oh I can't wait! 10, 9, 8, 7, 6, 5, 4, 3, 2, 1. 12." The room flashed for a second as a bang erupted. The bullet went straight through his skull.
"It's about time they were put to sleep. It's been repeating for months now," a figure in a lab coat said, writing in their notebook.

Tyler Barnes (12)

Ormiston Horizon Academy, Tunstall

2 Minutes

2 minutes. It doesn't seem very long, does it? But when your hair is knotted and your head's pinned back and facing a grey wall with a clock, when the bloody gash in your face kills you... 2 minutes seems like a lifetime, like you're in a boring lesson, time moves slowly. It's strange. You can hear the lonely voice in your head fade away. The second hand on the clock torments and tortures you until your death. The image of your best friend's sinister grin taunts you. How dare she betray you! Now look at you. No hope...

Sophie Beech (14)
Ormiston Horizon Academy, Tunstall

Taken At Room 404

My phone rang... not in my contacts. The number was 07799265***. I answered. The voice was deep.
He said, "Room 404 at 08:09, tomorrow."
Then he put the phone down. *Should I go? Why should I go? And who is he?* So many questions ran through my head at that moment. The next day came, it was 08:01, I had 8 minutes to get to room 404... I finally made it to room 404. I knocked, no reply. But a note slid under the door saying 'Turn around' written in blood. *Death. Stabbed. Killed. Taken...*

Charlotte Plant (13)
Ormiston Horizon Academy, Tunstall

10 Minutes

10 minutes, that's all I have left. 10 minutes. Never in my life have I thought 10 minutes could feel like hell My heart slowly beeps, my head hurts. The blaring lights shine down on me. My eyes begin to blur from tears. I can't believe this. I can't look at the clock. It feels like my heart is breaking. The cries from my family are not helping. The ticking of the clock is not helping. It feels like a ticking bomb. The tick echoes through my head. The heart monitor shows my family my last moments. 10 minutes pass...

Daisy Barnett (13)
Ormiston Horizon Academy, Tunstall

19/3/09

It was 19/3/09. I'd been driving for 19 minutes, 39 seconds and the scenery started to look familiar. I thought I was getting deja vu but I forgot about it since I didn't believe in it. Another 19 minutes, 39 seconds later I saw this woman standing there for the 3rd time so I started to get scared! I thought I was being tricked, but after happening for the 19th time I was getting annoyed. I checked the time and it was 19:39. I felt that the numbers 19 and 39 were following me everywhere. Now I knew they were...

Bethan Jones (13)
Ormiston Horizon Academy, Tunstall

Hide-And-Seek

The countdown began, 60 seconds until I had to hide from the monstrous monsters, the seekers, that'd search for me and all the hiders out there. If found you were *dead!* If you were lucky enough to survive you'd win over millions. My heart was racing, my life was on the line! I found my hiding spot in a corner and a tiny gap where I could see anything move. I heard something that made me jump, a seeker with a knife was there. I held my breath and closed my eyes. When I opened them I saw only darkness!

Keyarna Chinn-Shaw (13)
Ormiston Horizon Academy, Tunstall

12 8 13

I woke up, the same as I did every day, staring at the same plain white walls.

"Number 10," it announced, "this is your chance. One chance to get out."

"What?" I said, "30 years in this place and you're going to let me out?"

"On one condition," they announced.

"What? *What?*" I said hopefully.

"You must kill 12 8 13."

A screen dropped and so did my heart. I had to kill 12 8 13... My wife and daughter...

Amylee Colley (12)

Ormiston Horizon Academy, Tunstall

27th Of April

It was the worst day of my life, she was gone! It was the 27th of April, the day my life changed for the worse. It was a normal day until I was told about what had happened. I cried and cried. Weeping in despair and concern, we stood by her grave, placing flowers there for her. We were all lost. 27, the number we would all remember forever, hearing the number made me heartbroken. One day I heard the song, her song. It took me back to the day when we were wearing all black, saying goodbye to her...

Sienna-Mae Kinsey (12)
Ormiston Horizon Academy, Tunstall

My Special Day

My lucky number is 11 and it was a very special day as it was 11/11/2011. Also, it was about to strike 11 for a minute of silence to remember those who fought in the war. My friends and I were playing this bonkers board game. It hit 11 so we stood up and stopped talking. All I could hear were the gusts of wind which sounded like a tornado was appearing. The timer went off so we carried on playing this game and it was my turn. What a surprise! I got 11. What a special day it was.

Michaela Windsor (13)
Ormiston Horizon Academy, Tunstall

101

I had just robbed a bank. I thought I was getting away with £101k in cash but then I saw red and blue flashing lights, so I sped up from 30mph to 40 to 50. They got closer though so I went faster. I got to 90 to 91 to 98 to 100. I needed to go faster but I wouldn't get away, but I still tried. I went up to 101 and teleported to a dark, stormy area. I wasn't on Earth but a copy of Earth that had a red sky and it smelt of rotten flesh...

Lucas Hassall (12)

Ormiston Horizon Academy, Tunstall

Who Did It?

It was the summer of '69, on a Friday. My friend and I were excited about our murder mystery book when we got home. We were so excited.

"Help! Help! The teacher's been murdered!" someone suddenly yelled so everyone rushed to the body. It appeared that there was a pencil stabbed into his chest.

The police came and told us we couldn't touch the body. My friend and I decided to just look at the body but then we noticed that there was a piece of paper. It was our maths teacher's work. There was a whisper from behind me...

Logan Newman (12)
Radnor House Sevenoaks School, Sundridge

The Devil Rising

666. The number that represents the Devil. An angel cast out by God through his hatred of humans. He had to say goodbye to Heaven and hello to Hell! He now spends his time creating demons and princesses of Hell. One of his demons, Lillith, began breaking the 66 seal to free him from Hell. He didn't belong there anymore. Despite being almost successful, Lillith's plans were soon interrupted by Sam and Dean, the brothers of God. Who would be successful? Would Lucifer finally be free from Hell? Would the 66 seal be broken forever? You better say your prayers!

Cobie Nicholson (15)

Redcar & Cleveland College, Redcar

Then There Was 1

On 17th November 2022 a group of 10 friends met at the entrance of the desolate woodlands. Within seconds, 2 of the friends disappeared out of nowhere. No explanation. No goodbye. Nothing. Just completely gone. 5 days went by with still no sign. 5 days that felt like forever. To protect their safety the police blocked the group into a hotel but there was nothing safe about it. Day by day, one by one, another friend went missing. No explanation. No goodbye. Nothing. Just completely gone. I stood at the entrance of the woodland. "Take me too," I screamed.

Leah Ripley (16)
Redcar & Cleveland College, Redcar

5am

I woke up screaming because of a bad dream that my dad died. My husband lay next to me sound asleep, so I tried to do that too. In the morning my mother rang me screaming that my father was dead. That broke me. The dreams kept happening and more family kept dying and I kept feeling more broken every day. I had enough so I tried to kill myself, but it didn't work. So I shot my husband. It worked. I noticed that all the family deaths happened at 5am. I realised that I killed my husband at 5am...

Isla Hanlon (13)
Sawtry Village Academy, Huntingdon

Room 237 Was Empty

Room 237 was empty... It was where we were meant to meet. We were going to do the trade. In my ear, my partner told me that she had hacked the computers. The room was dark, but not dark enough for me to not see anything. Then I waited for them. I had to leave - I was there for too long... I flew back home. Then I went to the office. "The boss wants to see you," said Jasmin.
I knew that this was going to be bad. "You're not going to be on the field anymore," the boss said.

Olivia Smith (14)
St Columbanus' College, Bangor

I Rolled A 6

I roll a 6; two threes. I need a hard eight; two fours. I am in even more debt than I was before. I won at a casino once and ever since I... I can't stop. I have gambled my life away. I have gone too far...

It all started when me and a couple of friends had a, well, what we thought was an amazing idea. It was to go to a casino and gamble on our last night of college. Not going to lie, it went off with a bang! The night I won; I won a lot.

Ellie Gow (12)

St Columbanus' College, Bangor

Room 313

I open the door to my hotel room. I am in room 313, on the top floor. Panting after all those stairs, I decide to look around. This is probably the worst hotel in the area, cold, and the dustiest place ever. Coughing endlessly, I attempt to wipe away the dust. While I investigate my room, the sound of stone moving reaches my ears. I spin around to see a door which I enter. On the wall are words in red reading: 'Room 313. Always unoccupied'. Just then, the door closes, leaving me in darkness... The room, unoccupied once more...

Evie Bourne (12)
St John Henry Newman Catholic School, Carlisle

Room 23

She opened her eyes. She was lost, confused, sad, upset. She had no idea where she was, in a meticulous room with a door and a bed. It was room 23. She had vague light coming in from the keyhole in the door. She looked through it to find she was in the middle of an eerie forest. A sight that has stayed with her ever since. In front of her, trees stood forming the number 23. There was an eerie wind enveloping her, consuming her. The silence deafening her.

Conor Grew (14)

St Kevin's College, Lisnaskea

Number 11

Room 237 is empty; number 7 is gone. The intercom comes on and says he was caught outside of his room, so they took care of him. In our world, you don't have a name, you have a number. I'm number 11. How do you get here, you may ask? Well, this is a place for naughty children to stay, we live on one of the many moons of Jupiter, Amalthea. We're not allowed to communicate with other numbers or leave our rooms. But I'm starving as we only get fed once a day, I am going to sneak out...

Ava Matthews
Thamesmead School, Shepperton

My 20th

It was December 20th. I pranced out of my house and down the street in celebration, as today was my 20th birthday. My phone flooded with a plethora of messages. Ecstatically I read the heart-warming paragraphs sent by my friends as I crossed the road. Abruptly, my attention was shifted by a boisterous horn and bright lights.

That's all I can remember until the moment my eyes fluttered open to reveal a cemetery, coated with angelic snow. A fluorescent glow outlined a certain headstone. I limped over and gasped as my eyes met the carving on it: 'Naeema, 20/12/02-20/12/22'.

Naeema Mahmood (13)
Wigston Academy, Wigston

Noisy Neighbour

My neighbour Will had always been very suspiciously secretive and now I know why.

It all occurred the night before, behind the chilling door of 66. Blistering cold air and a scream of pure horror knocked at the walls separating me and next door. The scream echoed for around 10 seconds until it sharply stopped.

As the neighbourly thing to do, I finished watching my scary film and with all my confidence knocked faintly at door number 66.

"Hello, Annabelle," Will cried. *Smash!*

Now I know what happened behind door 66. All for the cost of my own death.

Esmee Durrant (14)
Wigston Academy, Wigston

All My Years

15 years. That was sufficient, and now I'd got my paycheck I should be able to buy that dress. Perfect!

"Here, I'm passing years to you," I heard my mum telling my sister after she spent all her years shopping. I always knew she was the favourite.

After breakfast, I got online and found the dress. Before pressing buy, I remembered my mum's voice: "It's dangerous to buy online, you could get scammed and lose all your years, but I won't help you."

I ignored the voice and bought it. I looked at my years. There were 15... hours...

Maia Westgarth Mestre (13)
Wigston Academy, Wigston

7pm On The Dot

I waited. 7pm was the time. No earlier, no later, no name, no context. 3 minutes until my fate was decided. I was counting down every single second, every millisecond, until I had to go.
All of a sudden the phone rang. I answered. "Get out of the car."
I could hear my heartbeat accelerating faster and faster until the silence was cut out by my shaky voice. "Okay."
I stepped out of my car thinking of any situation I could be put under, my brow dripping with sweat. I wiped it off, pulled myself together and lost all senses.

Leah Mistry (13)

Wigston Academy, Wigston

Isolated

I can't tell how long I've been stuck in this room for. I've started to lose my mind. Isolated in a dark room, with society just outside the non-existent window, for at least 48 hours. No one to talk to except the rats chewing on my shoes.

Then there's a sudden ringing in my ears like the ticking of a clock, getting faster and faster, louder and louder. It won't stop! I'm going insane! I don't know where it's coming from. There's no clock in the room!

No! This is it. This is the end. I'm going to die alone.

Allie Wolloff (14)
Wigston Academy, Wigston

2100

It was the year 2100. The human civil war had been going on for nearly a century, millions of lives lost, thousands of buildings turned into rubble. Food was in short supply. 2100 technology was very advanced. Guns turned people to ashes in one hit. Tanks were made of an indestructible metal called plasmanium.

I was charging into the bloodbath, knowing that all it took for me to die was one shot. All around me was misery, death and destruction.

Suddenly I felt a burning heat inside me. I had been shot. The year was 2100, the year I died.

Seth Orton (13)
Wigston Academy, Wigston

Escape

It was a dark, quiet night and there were 3 deadly, bloodthirsty murderers in the modern, white, colossal mansion and the only way for Mikey to escape was to get all the way to the ground floor and get in his rapid, black speedboat so he could escape his private island.

Mikey sprinted towards his huge balcony. He opened the huge glass doors as he heard the murderers stomp quickly up the stairs. He fell 3 whole floors into his massive garden pool and sprinted towards his black speedboat. He got in, turned the shiny keys and rapidly drove away.

Rhys Moon (13)
Wigston Academy, Wigston

1

Hello, I'm the best of the rest. I am 1. Some say my job is easy but it's very tough. People say that I am the easiest to learn but it's very different. Some numbers say that I'm the luckiest as I'm always first but as people get older the days get longer. Children's voices start to get annoying when you hear them all day every day.

Starting to go insane, I only want to get some sleep or some rest. I occasionally get some rest but it's not enough. I can't keep myself from depression. I am suffering sadness.

Riley Liquorish (14)
Wigston Academy, Wigston

1 Big Simulation

The year was 3078. Only half the universe remained. There was a big chemical blast that destroyed half of reality. Everywhere was damaged and deserted. The computer system had taken over. There was no way to escape the Matrix. All my family had died. The only thing I knew was that there was a massive explosion that destroyed almost everything, or could it not be real? Just one big simulation. I was running to my shelter this morning and I found a piece of paper on the floor saying that it was Russia that sent the explosion. I was shocked.

Jayden Williams (13)
Wigston Academy, Wigston

Christmas Thrill

2 hours to go, excitement fills me up like the happiness of a kid who has been thrown a big party for their birthday. A really short amount of time until I can open all the gifts for Christmas. Well, that's what my parents think anyway because I was peeking when they wrapped the gifts. I got the impatient gene from my mum I guess.

Although I'm excited I'm also pretty scared since I heard irritating rattling in one of the only 2 gifts I didn't open. Hopefully, it isn't a snake. I hate them with a passion.

Arihanna Joseph (13)
Wigston Academy, Wigston

The Last Moments

Only 10 seconds left until the world's biggest tsunami hits! 10. I search for shelter. 9. I look at the people trying to escape. 8. The city is getting robbed, looted and destroyed. 7. I look back at how my life could've been better. 6. I can hear the big tsunami making its way downtown. 5. I hear the screaming of poor people getting washed up and swallowed whole. 4. I hear the crash of cars, buses, trucks and other objects crashing into buildings and other objects. 3. I don't see a way out. 2. It's close! 1...

Logan Lewin (14)
Wigston Academy, Wigston

Time Was Gone

With only 30 seconds left I calculated the distance between me and the bus. 10 seconds left. I jumped. I was a public enemy and had managed to escape for now.

I arrived at the safe house. It was empty. No one in sight. Where did everyone go? As I ransacked the house for clues I realised I was in a simulation. Date, 2099, the future of Earth.

I kept on walking with a gun on my hip. There were agents in front. I shot repeatedly and there were none left.

I turned around. *Bang.* It was too late.

Ben Bessant (13)

Wigston Academy, Wigston

The Party

The party started at 13:00 on Friday 13th 2009. It was an unlucky number for some so surely the party was going to be horrific.

I knocked at the large brown door located on West Avenue Close, number 13. There was no answer. I was panicking like a fish in a flock of birds. Was I at the wrong house, wrong time or was it because of the number 13? My mind was racing.

Suddenly a black cab pulled up and shouted, "Get in!" I jumped straight in but I didn't know I was walking into a death trap.

Cadie Munday (13)
Wigston Academy, Wigston

The Code

2364... I was told on the radio that was the code. With every step, the door became clearer. I stood in front of the door with a slight glow on my face. I took a deep breath and typed the code... "2364," I muttered. I pressed 'enter' and the door slowly opened.

I walked into the room. It was empty. I turned on my torch and searched around in a panic. I moved my torch left and right, but there was nothing. I turned to leave but the door slammed shut. I knew I was trapped. It was the end.

Olivia Derry (13)
Wigston Academy, Wigston

The 3 Mischievous Sisters

It was the day, in 2022, my second oldest cat gave birth to 3 little, mischievous kittens. They loved each other. They went on adventures as they were born together at 6pm on June the 16th.

They have been separated since the 17th of August and never saw each other again. We have only 1 little, mischievous kitten now but she's very naughty. She does her business everywhere but she still has a great bond with her mother and she still misses her 2 sisters but they don't have a bond together anymore.

Harry Mansfield (11)
Wigston Academy, Wigston

I Am Number 14: Lucky For Some, Unlucky For Others

There I was, standing alone. All that I could hear were my deadly thoughts. In the corner of my eye, I suddenly saw something move. It was in room 4269. I had to check it out, was I not alone? I entered the room and looked around until the unexpected happened. Suddenly the door slammed closed and locked. *Click, click, click...* There were 30 seconds left. Panic started to rush into my head. No windows. No people. Just a silent room with no other exit. It was at that moment that I knew, it was the end.

Jenson Bentley (12)

Wigston Academy, Wigston

No Answer

I only had 40 seconds left. I was sweating all over. If I didn't do this what would happen? That's the thing, no one knows what happens if you don't answer this question. But I didn't know what the answer was or what the costs were. I thought and thought a lot but I was still clueless and I only had a little time left.

I finally had it! I knew the answer and I was nearly out of time! I told them what my answer was but I was incorrect. They started to take me somewhere... But where?

Charlotte Vann (13)
Wigston Academy, Wigston

The Legend

I found it. Finally, the number 666, carved into the grave with moss building over it as it had not been taken care of, left to mould in the hard, stable ground. It was around 2:45. It was dark and I was alone. The air stabbed into me, blowing my messy hair everywhere. I stood there waiting to see if the legend was true. I just needed to wait 10 more seconds.

10, 9, 8. I was petrified. 7, 6, 5. The trees leaned over, watching carefully. 4, 3, 2. Should I have done this? 1. I suddenly regretted it.

Beau Earl (14)

Wigston Academy, Wigston

7 Slaves

In Roman times, 7 years before the end of this reign of slavery, I'm the 7th slave. Number 7, a slave of the cruel mistress Freya of the Order of the Rose under the command of Princess Lyla, the daughter of Ollie the king of Derbyshire. Freya, being of a noble family, is quite snobby when it comes to slaves. She has 7 slaves, none of which are female. Freya is 17. She calls us the 7 slaves. We are all 7 years old. We fought in the colosseum for 7 days straight and on the 7th day I died.

Ollie Derbyshire (11)

Wigston Academy, Wigston

The Real Game Of Life

I roll a 6. This means I can go forward 6 spaces. I look back and see all the other people behind. As I get closer to the end, every time I move one more space I know I'm closer to leaving and all the people behind me are getting lost. I have to make the biggest decision ever.

As I sweat to take a step, I decide to let the 5 people behind take my steps. I'll fall but at least they'll live. I help them all through.

When the last person rolls the dice, I say my goodbyes.

Zaynab Okba (13)
Wigston Academy, Wigston

Out Of Money

It is 2016 and a new rule has been made. If you run out of money you will disappear to get rid of people. "The world is overpopulated."

I only have £15 and that has got to last me the rest of the year, and robberies have increased. Things are so expensive and I'm starting to panic because I'm too young to die. I run out of money and a title over my head says *Error*. I start to cry. Is this it for me? I decide to accept my fate and enjoy the afterlife.

Imogen Shipley (11)
Wigston Academy, Wigston

The Day

One day at home I was watching the football when I thought football was my passion. I went in my garden, trying to kick a ball. Finally, the day came when I kicked the ball around 1 metre. I kicked it again and it went nowhere. I went to a football team. I was so scared. I got partnered up with another girl. She was so good. My number was 4. I stepped on the pitch for the first time. I kicked the ball in the air and scored.
I went back home. But it was all a dream.

Isabelle Wall (12)
Wigston Academy, Wigston

My Life In 12

I'm nearly 12. I can't wait. 12 is my lucky number. It's not long after Christmas, just 3 weeks. There's not long to go so this is the start.

12 is not old. I'm not an adult yet, so I need to make the most of it. I'm not young forever, so I need to have fun whilst I'm young. Being an adult is hard work (because I get told), too hard for me so I need to make the most of it, you see.

Seth Clamp (11)
Wigston Academy, Wigston

Rocket 70

I still remember that day. The unholy day when failure happened. It was a very rainy day and it dribbled down my head onto my leather boots. The 3 fearless astronauts boarded with passion. Everybody was happy.
"3, 2, 1, blast off!"
But then it happened. I saw everything. I saw the towers collapse. I saw the collision. But I didn't see the astronauts. That was the disaster of Rocket 70.

Matthew Marriott (11)
Wigston Academy, Wigston

Ransom

It was 2022. I worked in a hotel. I got a letter in the post today. I opened it. I was so scared and shaky. I took a big breath and looked. It said 'If you want your daughter back, call this number: 07197619***'.
I was unsure if I wanted to call the number. I thought and thought. The more and more I thought the more nervous I got. I thought for 4 hours and I decided to call the number.

Lily Horton (12)
Wigston Academy, Wigston

Number 13

I looked down at my hand to see the number 13. *Why's the number 13 on my hand?* As the day went on, I kept seeing the number everywhere. *Why number 13?* I thought to myself. *It's supposed to be unlucky and now I'm stuck with it, even though I don't really believe that.*
I tried to do some research, but couldn't find anything. I suddenly got tired and couldn't be bothered to search anymore. When I woke up, I wasn't at home. *What is going on? No one is around.* I was stuck. *I guess 13 is really unlucky.*

Freya Mower (16)
Wilberforce College, Hull

History-Makers Or Not?

There are only 30 seconds left. A chance to make history. Senegal have the chance to be the first African nation to win the World Cup. They lead Portugal by 1 goal to nil. A fairy-tale story for this nation coming back from a 4-1 deficit to lead 5-4, it has been truly magnificent. All Senegal have to do is defend like they have never done before for 30 additional seconds and they will be history-makers. Ronaldo has a penalty. Maybe the greatest scorer can deny them? It's the final kick of the match. Ronaldo misses! Senegal have won.

Oliver Rigg (17)
Wilberforce College, Hull

The Haunted House

Ping! I received a message from an unknown number telling me to follow the route they were sending. As I reached the destination, I arrived at a house. It wasn't an ordinary house, it was a haunted house!

As I entered the house and looked around, I realised I wasn't the only 1 there. As a few more arrived, I started to feel very cautious about what was going on. *Boom!* The doors were locked, windows barricaded. No way out. It was like we were being used for a project. As I turned my head, I saw them. Oh no...

Millie Richards (17)

Wilberforce College, Hull

Experiment 101

Room 237 was empty... No, no, no! Damn it. I punched the wall with anger and worry. Experiment 101 was out of the room, which was a horrific sign. Experiment 101 was a little girl with huge power who could kill. It worried me as a sister to her, but also as a scientist. I promised 101 that she'd be fine and would survive but because of all the tests, she was sick of them. She hated them, she hated everyone. She hated me... I missed her. I wanted her back.
"I'm so sorry, it's all my fault, Experiment 101."

Julia Pawlowski (16)
Wilberforce College, Hull

My Secret At 16...

I was hated by everyone in the village because of a reason I only found out when I was 16. I had a powerful monster inside me that once destroyed the village and as I was walking, I got taken to the owner of the village. They said they would have to kill me. As they started to grab me with force, I suddenly felt anger boiling up. It was so painful, almost like I was being burnt alive.
I started screaming, "It hurts! It hurts! Help me!"
My skin started to peel off and I turned into the beast...

Guilherme Barroso (17)
Wilberforce College, Hull

The Last 20 Seconds...

Only 20 seconds left and I can feel the world about to crash down on me like piles of hailstones on a stormy day. I can't breathe or anything because I know me and everyone else on this planet are about to die in the worst way possible. The time is just ticking so fast with only 10 seconds left and then everyone's life will be over and done. I wish I could spend this last time with my family but there is no time for that because the time is over.
With just a second left, goodbye everyone...

Ellis Rennie (17)
Wilberforce College, Hull

The Last Survivor

I was the only 1 left, everyone else had been killed by those relentless demons. It was up to me to save the world from this world-splitting disaster. But no matter how many demons I killed, more just kept coming up from the depths of Hell. I had to figure out a way to close up the gateway that was letting these demons create havoc. It took me all night to think of a plan. I just had to find a way to execute my plan. Just as I was about to execute my plan, I was interrupted...

Luis Witty (16)
Wilberforce College, Hull

The End?

I was down to my last £5. My heart skipped a beat and my palms turned sweaty. *How am I going to survive? I can't, there's no way I can survive.* I got my phone out and my hands were shaking like a leaf on a windy day. I dialled the number, 999. Before I could even say the word help, the phone cut. My eyes brightened. I stood in fear, thinking and repeating to myself that this could be the end. I mean the end of everything, absolutely everything.

Cecilia Mukelenge (16)
Wilberforce College, Hull

2099

I opened my eyes and found myself on the ship. I didn't know anything about my past. The robot came out and carried me outside the ship. I wasn't able to move my head because I was frozen. My beard and moustache had grown, but I was feeling like a child. I couldn't remember anything about my past but I knew how I felt as a child. When the robot carried me outside the ship, I saw a card with the date on it. 19th May 2099. I realised I had been resurrected.

Can Yildiz (17)
Wilberforce College, Hull

YOUNG WRITERS INFORMATION

We hope you have enjoyed reading this book – and that you will continue to in the coming years.

If you're the parent or family member of an enthusiastic poet or story writer, do visit our website www.youngwriters.co.uk/subscribe and sign up to receive news, competitions, writing challenges and tips, activities and much, much more! There's lots to keep budding writers motivated!

If you would like to order further copies of this book, or any of our other titles, then please give us a call or order via your online account.

Young Writers
Remus House
Coltsfoot Drive
Peterborough
PE2 9BF
(01733) 890066
info@youngwriters.co.uk

Join in the conversation!
Tips, news, giveaways and much more!

 YoungWritersUK  YoungWritersCW  youngwriterscw

Scan me to watch the Integer video!